"My mother said to keep a close eye on my preschool triplet cousins while she ran an errand, and I said I would. And I will, just as soon as I *find* them."

Danny only left Suzy, Sally, and Sammy alone for a few minutes, but when he came back, the girls were gone. Being in charge wasn't quite as exciting as Danny had expected. . . .

Elspeth Campbell Murphy

DANNY PETROWSKI

Illustrated by Tony Kenyon

Smile
God Loves
YOU **Lucile's**

Christian Supplies
And Hobbies Center

Box 187 893-4641 AKRON, INDIANA 46910

Chariot Books
DAVID C. COOK PUBLISHING CO.

Chariot Books is an imprint of David C. Cook Publishing Co.
David C. Cook Publishing Co., Elgin, Illinois 60120
David C. Cook Publishing Co., Weston, Ontario

DANNY PETROWSKI
© 1985 by Elspeth Campbell Murphy

Illustrated by Tony Kenyon
Cover and book design by Catherine Hesz

First Printing, 1985
Printed in the United States of America
90 89 88 87 86 85   5 4 3 2 1

Library of Congress Cataloging in Publication Data

Murphy, Elspeth Campbell.
  Danny Petrowski

  Summary: In the prayer journal he keeps as part of a Sunday school project, Danny
reveals his lack of self-confidence and how he comes to realize that he is a talented
and worthwhile person.
  [1. Self-perception—Fiction. 2. Conduct of life—Fiction. 3. Christian life—Fiction]
I. Kenyon, Tony, ill. II. Title.
PZ7.M95316Dan   1985   [Fic]   85-16568
ISBN 0-89191-730-6

*For the Schroeder family
with love*

WEEK 1

Saturday

Dear God,

I'm writing this in the library. It seems funny to be praying here, but that's what I'm doing—I'm talking to you by writing in this new notebook. Miss Jenkins, my Sunday school teacher, told us we should try keeping prayer journals, and she even bought us notebooks to get us started. She said it would be something like writing letters to you. I would rather draw than write, but writing is OK, too, and I like starting a new notebook.

Today it's raining, so my friend Pug and

I are spending the whole afternoon in the library. Pug takes forever in the library, because he has to look at every science book on the shelf. But that's OK, because we have to wait for my mom to come get us anyway.

Before I started writing this, I looked all through a big book that was lying on the table. It was all about parrots. I never saw so many beautiful colors. They reminded me of all the crayons and colored pencils and paints I have at home. I wonder if real birds really come in those colors—or is it a trick of the camera?

While I was waiting for Pug, I thought it would be fun to pick out my favorite parrots. So that's what I did. And then Pug still wasn't ready, so I thought it would be fun to pick out my *very* favorite parrot. So I did that, too. I even wrote the name down.

8

It's called a Scarlet Macaw. It has a red head and a red body. It has yellow and blue and green on its wings. And it has blue on its tail. I can't check the book out and take it home, because it's from the adult section and I only have a children's card.

I wish I could draw a Scarlet Macaw. But I just now tried to, and it didn't come out right. You must be really smart, God, to make a real bird that beautiful. I can't even draw one.

Pug finally got in line to check out his books. So I guess I will go now. We'll wait by the door for my mom to drive up in the car. She'll honk, and we'll zip our books inside our jackets and make a run for it. But we'll still get wet.

Pug is coming over to my house for supper. Every time he comes over he says the same thing. He says, "Wow! Is your house ever quiet. It's great. No dumb girls giggling and yelling at you. No telephone ringing every two seconds." I never used to think my house was quiet until Pug said that, but I guess it is. Pug has a bunch of older sisters. I can never remember how old they are or what their names are. I'm not even sure Pug can.

There's one younger girl, Cindy, too. She likes to hang around with us. Sometimes we let her, but Pug tells her it's on one condition: that she does what we tell her and doesn't bother us or talk. So it works out OK for everyone. Pug doesn't like being the only boy in his family.

My father keeps telling me that I'm his favorite child, but that's not as great as it seems since there are no other kids in my family besides me. Except when my cousins come to stay with us. Then I'm not the only child.

My cousins are triplets, and their names are Suzy, Sally, and Sammy. When Pug first heard about them, he said, "Well, at least one of them is a boy." But I said, "No, Sammy is short for Samantha." They are all the same age, because they are triplets. And they're not old enough for school yet. And sometimes they drive me crazy, God! Now Pug is waving at *me* to hurry up. How do you like that? But I guess I'd better go now.

Love,
Danny

Sunday

Dear God,

It's the next day now, and I just read the stuff I wrote to you yesterday. It was a funny kind of prayer, I think. Reason Number One, because it was written down. And Reason Number Two, because I wrote it down in the library with all these people around. And Reason Number Three, because I didn't ask you for anything. I guess maybe there are different kinds of prayers. I guess it's OK just to tell you how things are going with me.

I guess it's good to thank you for things, too. Pastor Bennett says we should remember to thank you for people. My mother always thanks you for Suzy, Sally, and Sammy, but I don't know about that. I think Pug would be a good person to thank you for, because he's my best friend.

Pug is an orangehead. I don't know why people say redheads have red hair when it's really orange hair, do you? Pug has bright orange hair and freckles and a small, turned-up nose. That's where he got his nickname—from his pug nose. His real name is Philip, but no one ever calls him that. When Pug was just a baby, his big sisters started calling him Pug. Then other people started, and then I guess no one could stop. But Pug doesn't seem to care. Maybe having a pug nose is not the same thing as being fat.

I think I'm fat, but my mother says I'm not fat—I'm just not-thin. I would hate it if someone started calling me Tubs or Fats. I hope no one ever gets the idea to do that. I hope my parents never adopt an older sister, because she might get together with Pug's sisters and think up a name for me.

14

Pug has another nickname for when the other kids aren't calling him Pug, and that is the Mad Scientist. Pug doesn't mind being called that, either. In fact, if you want to know the truth, I think he likes it, because he wants to be a scientist.

Sometimes I worry what would happen if I didn't have Pug for a best friend. But he is still my best friend, so I would like to say thank you for him.

Love,
Danny

Monday
Dear God,

You know what I've been thinking about all day long? I've been thinking about that Scarlet Macaw I saw in the library book the other day. And that gave me an idea. I thought it would be great to have a bird like that. You know, to buy it. I could put

15

the cage in my room so that the first thing I would see in the morning would be those beautiful feathers. And I would teach it to say, "Good morning, Danny," and maybe to sing "O Danny Boy," which my father sings in the shower.

I don't know how much a Scarlet Macaw costs, but I think I probably have enough money. The book said they were relatively inexpensive. I had saved up $4.79, and then I got $10.00 for birthday money. So when I put my old money and my new money together, I have $14.79. Someday soon I think I'll walk home from school a different way, so I can stop by the pet store. I'll see how much a Macaw costs, and then I'll ask my mother if I can spend my money on it.

Love,
Danny

Tuesday
Dear God,

I'm writing this from my grandmother's house. I didn't get to go to the pet store, because my mom picked me up after school and we drove to my grandmother's, which is in another town. There aren't any kids around here, so I have to bring stuff to do. I brought my drawing pad and my colored pencils and this notebook. I already drew some things, so I am writing now. My mother and grandmother are still downstairs drinking tea and talking. My grandmother is from England, so she drinks tea a lot.

When I'm here, I like to look out this window at the spooky old empty house across the street. I drew a picture of the house in my pad. Tomorrow I'll show it to Pug and see what he thinks. I would like

17

to go inside the house, but I don't think I'd like to go by myself.

I'm trying to think of some kids that would be good to look at a spooky house with. There are the kids in my Sunday school class. You already know who they are, God, because you know all about everyone. But I will write their names down: Pug McConnell, Curtis Anderson, Mary Jo Bennett, Julie Chang, and Becky Garcia.

Pug would be a good one to take in the house, because he'd be scared like me, but he would pretend that neither of us was scared at all and that we were on some kind of scientific expedition. We'd still be scared, but pretending not to be scared is almost as good sometimes as not being scared at all.

Then there's Mary Jo Bennett. She has never been scared of anything in her whole life. She is the bravest, noisiest, fastest, craziest kid you ever saw. Pastor Bennett is her father, and he calls her the wild child. All the ladies at church, who don't really know her, think Mary Jo is the sweetest, most delicate little thing in the world. That's because she is short for her age and very pretty. Nothing makes Mary Jo madder than when people think she is little and cute, though.

Mary Jo is nice, but the problem is—she is so brave, she makes other people feel like chickens. If she went in the spooky house with you, she'd keep saying, "Come on. Come *on!*" She'd even go running down to see what was in the basement and make you go, too.

Then there's Julie. When my school-teacher, Mrs. Whitney, has a sub, she always leaves Julie and Curtis in charge,

19

because she says they're so responsible. Julie has the neatest desk in the whole class. Sometimes Mrs. Whitney makes the rest of us gather around to look at it. Julie always has an extra sharpened pencil. But if you break yours or lose it, she's nice about sharing with you. She doesn't say, "Tough luck," or anything like that.

But Julie would complain that the spooky house was dirty. And she'd say that the floor might be rotted and you could fall through. Or that plaster from the ceiling might drop on your head. Julie is nice, but sometimes she acts too much like a grown-up.

There is this other boy in my Sunday school class named Curtis. Curtis would be good to have for another best friend, but I don't know him very well. When you made people, God, I think you put more stuff into some of them than into others. Curtis has a lot of stuff in him. I mean, he is so good at *everything*. He is learning to play the guitar, and he even played in church one Sunday night. And everyone smiled and nodded and whispered to each other about how good he is. People always seem surprised when kids are good at stuff.

Curtis is good at baseball, too. And he can run the fastest of anyone, except for Mary Jo. He is tall for his age and not a bit fat, and he goes to the next grade for reading. If I were Curtis, I wouldn't worry about anything.

So maybe the spooky house wouldn't bother Curtis. I don't know. But I think that even if Curtis were so scared he couldn't move, he would still make himself finish going through the whole house.

I almost forgot one other person, and

21

that is Becky. I probably almost forgot her because Becky is so quiet and shy. Becky doesn't like to get called on in school or Sunday school. But she still knows a lot of things, because she reads so much. I don't know if the stuff she knows is the same as the teacher is asking, but sometimes Becky surprises people with how much she knows, those times when she talks. Becky would be even more scared than I would. But that might be good after all, because then I wouldn't be the most scared one. I would seem brave.

I guess the best person to take in that spooky old house across the street would be Pug, which is who I started with in the first place.

My mother and grandmother must be finished drinking tea and talking, because my mother just called upstairs and said it's

22

time to go. So I won't write anymore now. My hand hurts, I've been writing so much. It's a funny thing, God. It used to be I could never think of enough things to say when I prayed. But look how long this letter is!

Love,
Danny

Wednesday
Dear God,

Yesterday as we were leaving my grandmother's house, guess what she gave me. A new box of sixty-four crayons! It wasn't my birthday or Christmas or anything. She just did it to be nice, because she knows I like crayons and that I needed some new ones. Usually when I pray to you I say, "God bless Grandma." But when I think of Grandma, I'm not sure that's enough to say, only I don't know what else to say.

When my grandmother gave me the crayons, I pushed back the lid right away to take the biggest, longest, deepest breath I could. Nothing smells as good as crayons, God. I like to breathe in as hard as I can, as if I could sort of swallow the smell of the crayons through my nose. My grandmother laughed when I did that, like she thought I was the neatest kid in the world or something and that she was glad I was her grandson. So maybe when I say, "God bless Grandma," I will try to remember how she looked just then.

I've seen my mother take a big sniff when she opens a new can of coffee. Coffee is funny. I think it smells good, but it tastes awful. Of course, crayons taste worse than coffee, but then you're not supposed to eat crayons at all. My mother said when I was a baby, you couldn't put me

24

down anywhere near crayons, because I loved them so much I would try to eat them. Maybe I was just trying to swallow the smell the same as now.

I think you had good ideas when you made people able to see colors and to smell crayons, God. I like the feel of crayons, too. Sometimes I take all the crayons out of the box and then put them back in with all the blues together and then all the reds and the greens and the yellows. Then I take them out of the box again and match up the colors I think look pretty together. Sometimes I forget how much time is going by, and I think it's not time for supper when it really is.

I have to stop writing now, because I have a job to do. I learned that crayons last longer if you wrap masking tape around them, so that's what I'm going to do. My father doesn't like it when I play with the masking tape, because then he can never find it. But this is a good reason, so he will say OK.

Looking at the colors in my crayon box reminded me of the colors on the Scarlet Macaw. It was the first thing I drew with my new crayons, but the picture still doesn't look right. I think tomorrow will be a good day to go to the pet store. It's funny how the more you think about a thing sometimes the more you want it.

Love,
Danny

Thursday
Dear God,

Miss Jenkins, our Sunday school teacher, said we should tell you about our feelings and that you would always understand. She said that no one can be happy all the time and that sad feelings are OK to have. Well, God, I hope you understand *dumb* feelings, because that's how I feel now.

Remember, yesterday, I was talking about going to the pet store? I felt so good then. It's funny how you can feel good one day and awful the next. I went to the pet store today. But I will start at the beginning and just tell you what happened, OK?

Well, first of all, Pug and I went there after school, and we saw this sign on the door that said: *Children Under 14 Must Be Accompanied by an Adult.* I guess they have that sign because they're afraid kids will run around and wreck stuff. But Pug and I wouldn't do that. I think kids who don't wreck things should be allowed to go places. Well, anyway, Pug and I didn't

27

have an adult, and we were trying to figure out how to get one, when the salesclerk came to the door. I think maybe he was the manager. He asked if there was something in particular we wanted, and I took a deep breath and spoke right up and said, "Yes."

He said we could come in and look around as long as we didn't tap on the aquariums or put our fingers in the cages.

Right away Pug went off to look at the snakes and lizards. And that was OK with me, because in a way it was easier to tell the man what I wanted without someone else hearing. So I took a deep breath again and asked him if he had any Scarlet Macaws, because I wanted to find out how much they cost, because I wanted to buy one.

I had been practicing saying that in my head all day, and I was glad when it came

out all right. But it was funny to hear something with my ears that I'd only been hearing in my head before.

The man looked a little surprised when I told him what I wanted, but he took me over to the aisle where all the squawking was coming from. We went past the parakeets and canaries.

And suddenly, God, there it was! A real, live Scarlet Macaw. It was so beautiful it almost hurt my eyes to look at it. It was like my eyes couldn't really see all that color. Remember I said I didn't know if birds could really look as good as they did in the book? Well, they look *better!* I thought the library book had gotten me ready for what a Macaw would look like. But nothing could. I just stared at the Macaw, and it looked back at me.

The man talked to me like I was a grown-up customer. He said, "This is an especially fine Macaw, and he's already been tamed, so he's selling for eighteen hundred dollars."

And this is the dumb part, God. I said to him, "Did you say $18.00?" (Because I knew I only had $14.79, and that wouldn't be enough.)

And he laughed. Not a mean laugh, but kind of gentle laugh. He said, "No, eighteen *hundred* dollars. You know. A thousand plus eight hundred more."

The funniest thing happened, God. I could feel my mouth moving, but no sound came out, until finally my voice came out all squeaky and I said, "But—but that's almost two thousand dollars."

"Pretty close," the man said. "Some birds cost a lot more than two thousand dollars."

I could feel my face getting all hot, and my throat got all tight and sore. I felt so stupid and so disappointed all at the same time.

There was the most beautiful thing I'd ever seen—looking right at me—and it cost more money than I would ever have. Maybe some grown-ups have eighteen hundred dollars, but I don't know any kids who do.

31

After he told me how much the Macaw cost, the man asked if I would like to see it up close and even pet it. I couldn't believe the man would let me do that, because I'm sure he knew I didn't have enough money. But he kept on treating me like a grown-up. Before I could say anything, the man reached into the Macaw's cage, and the Macaw stepped off its perch and rode out on the man's arm. I reached out my hand and got to touch those soft, bright feathers.

The Macaw liked it when I talked to him and petted the back of his head. I was a little scared when I saw the Macaw up close; I think really good things are like that sometimes. They're good, but they're a little scary, too.

Just then Pug came over and all he said was, "Wow!" He got to pet the Macaw, too. Then the man put the Macaw back in the cage, and we said good-bye to the Macaw and thanked the man. He said if I really wanted a pet bird, I could start off with a parakeet. But he didn't pester me about it, because I think he knew it's hard to settle for a parakeet when what you really wanted was a Scarlet Macaw.

So that's what happened, God. I felt really dumb. But I've been thinking about the pet store manager. I'm glad he was so nice. He didn't have to be, but he still was. I think that's the way you would be, God, if you had a pet store, and some kid came in asking dumb questions. You would know the questions were dumb, even if the kid didn't. But you wouldn't make the kid feel dumb. I think that's the way it is when people pray to you, God. Maybe some of the prayers sound dumb. But you don't make people feel dumb at all.

You listen carefully, just like the man in the store, and you care about what's important to people. I don't know why you do all that, but I'm glad you do, anyway. Well, I really wrote a lot. I still feel dumb, but I don't feel as dumb as I did before.

Love,
Danny

WEEK 2

Sunday

Dear God,

Remember how Thursday I felt so dumb? Well, something nice happened today to make me feel not-so-dumb.

Sometimes things happen that way. First something bad happens, and then something good. Of course, a lot of the times it's bad—and then more bad. And sometimes it's good—and then more good. But good, then more good doesn't happen very often, so I'll settle for bad and then good.

I told you about Julie before. Well, if you

35

just looked at Julie, you'd think, "Here is a person who can do anything." Well, the thing is—Julie can't draw. Julie is a little bit crazy when it comes to cats, she likes them so much. But she can't draw them. And I can.

There are five cats at Julie's house, but her favorite is a little kitten named Oreo—which seems like a funny name for a cat, except his head and tail are mostly black and his middle is white, and he reminded Julie of an Oreo cookie. So that's why she named him Oreo.

Julie lives on my block, and yesterday I went to her house and she made Oreo sit still while I drew a picture of him. Actually it wasn't hard to make Oreo sit still, because he was asleep the whole time. Julie liked the picture so much she gave me a nickel. And that was the first time I ever

sold a picture. I knew people bought pictures, but I didn't know I would ever sell one of mine. I like being an artist!

This morning Julie told me that when Oreo finally woke up, she showed him the picture I drew of him and right away he knew who it was. But I said, "Julie, Oreo is just a cat. How do you know he could recognize himself in a picture?" And she said, "How do you know he couldn't? He's a very smart cat." I couldn't think of anything else to say, and I guess you shouldn't argue with people about their cats. Julie says cats are the best thing you ever made. No offense, God, but I don't think cats are. I think Scarlet Macaws are. I only wish I could get my drawing of one to come out right.

Love,
Danny

Monday

Dear God,

I hope you can read my handwriting, because I am writing this in a hurry. Sometimes I just seem to run out of time. And I don't really understand how that happens. Today, when the other kids saw Julie's picture of Oreo that I drew for her, I got a lot more orders for pictures. I said I would draw the new pictures tonight and bring them in tomorrow.

But this afternoon Pug and I went hunting for stuff to add to our collections. That's one of our favorite things to do, and we do it together. Today we decided to look for feathers on the ground. If we found something else that we liked we could keep it—it wasn't against the rules—but we were supposed to look for feathers.

I found some, and when I got home I

39

made a mobile out of them to hang in my room. Pug found some feathers, too, but he glued them on a sheet of paper for his feather book. He looked up in his science book to find out what kind they were, and he printed the names in his best printing.

Then Pug had to go home, and I started to work on the drawings the kids wanted me to do. The stuff they want is pretty easy. I really wanted to practice making a

Scarlet Macaw, but I decided I could do it later. I got so busy I didn't want to quit when my mom called me for supper. My parents have his rule that I can't bring my drawing pad and crayons to the table. So tonight I brought my drawing pad and *colored pencils* to the table. That didn't work, of course. I didn't really think it would, but I thought it was worth a try.

I wanted to watch television after supper, so I did—even though I still had more pictures to draw. I like to draw more than anything else, and I never thought I would get tired of it—but that's sort of how I felt. Now I wish I hadn't watched television, because if I hadn't, the drawings would be done.

My father just came by my door and saw the light on. He told me to turn the light off and go to sleep, because it's way past my bedtime. I guess I'd better, or he'll let me have it. But if I go to school tomorrow without the pictures, the kids might let me have it. Sometimes, God, it feels like no matter what you do, somebody's going to let you have it. I'm glad I can tell you how I feel and you know what I'm talking about.

Love,
Danny

Tuesday
Dear God,

Well, as you can see, nobody let me have it. Sometimes some of the bad things I think are going to happen for sure don't happen at all. I took the pictures that were finished to school, and the kids paid me for them. The other kids were disappointed that I didn't have theirs done, but I promised I would bring them in tomorrow, and they just said OK. I felt so glad that I didn't get in trouble, that the whole day turned out good.

Do you know what people mean when they say they feel blue? I do. It means they feel sad and kind of worn out. But I don't understand that, really. How can people have a bad day and call it "blue," when blue is such a good color?

To me a blue day is a day like today. Everything is bright and clear, and there are no clouds. And the sky is so blue and bright it almost hurts your eyes to look at it.

So if I tell you I feel blue today, you'll know what I mean, OK, God? You always understand what I mean, even if no one else does. When I feel blue, I mean I'm so happy I want to jump as high as I can and go swimming in the sky.

Love,
Danny

Wednesday
Dear God,

Today we had a fire drill. We had to get in line and march outside. It's a little bit like recess, except you can't run around.

You know what, God? Sometimes I make up these stories in my head. I don't tell them to anyone—not even Pug—but I tell them to myself. And I like them, because I get to be the hero in charge.

Like—what if there were a real fire, but Mrs. Whitney had a heart attack or something? Everybody would be scared, but I would get them all lined up and pick a couple of kids to drag Mrs. Whitney out-

44

side, and we would all get out OK. And later the principal and the firemen would tell me how glad they were that I knew the fire route and paid attention at fire drills and that I used the north door the way our wing is supposed to.

But I don't know if I will ever get to be the hero, God; it hasn't happened yet. Curtis is always automatically in charge of the boys, and Julie is always automatically in charge of the girls. But probably if there were a real fire, everyone would automatically follow Mary Jo and jump out the window.

Just once I would like to be in charge and be the hero. So far, I'm just an ordinary kid. It's a good thing you like ordinary kids.

Love,
Danny

Thursday

Dear God,

This afternoon in school Mrs. Whitney gave us free time. I asked her if I could paint. She said it was a lot of trouble to set out the easel and put newspapers on the floor. But I guess she could tell I really wanted to, so she said OK as long as I was careful to clean up. Sometimes I wonder why teachers and parents always have to add things like that. I think they should wait to see if you're really not going to clean up before they remind you to do it. But anyway, I promised I would clean up.

I didn't even know what I was going to make, but my hands just reached for the red, blue, yellow, and green paint. And then I started making the Scarlet Macaw. I had tried and tried to draw him before, and it never came out right. But for some

46

reason it came out right today. I got so busy working on the picture I almost forgot where I was.

It was funny, God. As I was working on my picture, I had two feelings hitting up against each other. It hurt to look at the painting I was making because it reminded me that I would probably never get a real Scarlet Macaw. But I could see that this was turning into one of my best pictures ever. So I was sad and excited all at the same time. How do you figure that out?

When the picture was pretty close to being done, Mrs. Whitney said free time was over because it was time to get ready to go home. I was almost done, so I begged her to give me a little more time and said that I would stay after school to clean up. She said OK and that she could tell it was important to me. But some of the other kids kept saying, "Mrs. Whitney, Danny's still painting" or "Isn't Danny going home?"

Honestly. Some people don't like things to be even a little bit different from the way they always are. But I kept painting even after the bell rang and the other kids went home. It felt funny being in the room with all the kids gone, except for Pug, who hung around waiting for me. Here I was, staying after school—not because I was in trouble or anything. Finally I was done, and my painting was beautiful. Mrs. Whitney said it was superb. I like that word—superb.

Mrs. Whitney said I should leave the painting overnight at school so it would dry. I didn't want to. It's hard to leave something when you want to take it home. I thought if I carried it very carefully the

48

49

paint wouldn't smear. But it had started to drizzle outside, so I decided I'd better leave my picture after all. Pug helped me clean up the paints, because if he'd stayed after school working on science, I would have waited for him and helped him clean up.

We left just as some other teachers were coming in for a committee meeting in our classroom. They looked funny scrunched down in kids' desks.

I felt *blue*, God. Remember what I think that means? Only not wild blue. Kind of quiet blue, with a little bit of green mixed in. I felt so good about my painting that even the ordinary things I was going to do after school seemed special and exciting, too. I wonder if this is what it feels like to be a hero. I didn't do anything brave, but I felt like Danny was a pretty good person to be. I wonder if Curtis feels this way all the time. I think it would feel weird to feel this good all the time. But it sure is nice sometimes. Hallelujah. That's another good word. Of course, you know it means Praise the Lord.

Love,
Danny

Friday
Dear God,

You'll never guess what happened today. But wait a minute. That's a funny thing to say to you, since you don't have to guess about anything—you just know it. Anyway, Mr. Collins, one of the upstairs teachers, stopped by to talk to Mrs. Whitney for a minute. We were doing seat work at our desks, but everybody looks up whenever another teacher comes into the room, and some kids automatically start talking, even though they're not supposed to. Then Mrs. Whitney called me up to her desk. Everybody stopped whispering and stared at me like I'd turned into a giant rabbit or something.

Pug caught my eye and raised his eyebrows real high as if he were asking me, "What's going on?" I just shrugged and raised my eyebrows real high, too, as if I were saying, "Beats me."

I guess I was a little bit scared, because whenever a teacher who's not yours wants to talk to you, you never know, you might be in trouble. But I didn't think I'd done anything wrong lately. And it turned out I wasn't in trouble at all.

This is the exciting part, God. Mr. Collins had seen my Macaw painting when he came to the committee meeting in our room yesterday afternoon, and he really liked my painting. He came to ask me if I wanted to join the after-school art club. I said I thought it was only for kids in the upper grades. Mr. Collins said it was, but that he thought I would be able to keep up.

He gave me a permission slip to bring back if I decide to join and a list of supplies. (Even though there aren't any dues or anything, the kids have to buy some of their own stuff.) I would have to stay after school two nights a week starting next week. Mr. Collins said that even though the club is fun it is still hard work, but he would like to have me.

And on top of all that, I got to take my painting home today.

Hallelujah! Blue!

Love,
Danny

Saturday

Dear God,

I am trying to decide about the after-school art club. I really want to do it, but I'm scared, too. I asked Mrs. Whitney and my parents what they thought I should do. They said it's up to me. Why is it that sometimes when you don't want to be told what to do, people tell you anyway. But then when you *do* want to be told what to do, they say, "It's up to you."

You know what I figured out, God? I think that when you have a chance to do something neat, you should probably do it. If you wait for a time to come when you won't be scared, you'll probably have to wait forever, because there probably won't ever be a time when you're not scared. And besides, if you wait too long, the neat chance might not even be there anymore.

54

Does that make sense, God? Do you know what I think? I think maybe being asked to join the art club is like a present from you. I'm going to join the art club.

LATER

Dear God,

This afternoon my dad and I did something special. We went to a real art supplies store to buy the things I need for the club. Mostly I just buy my art stuff in the art aisle of the toy store, but the toy store didn't have some of the things I needed. So we went to the art store, and I wandered up and down the aisles just looking and looking.

I saw my father look at his watch a couple of times, as if he couldn't believe how long I was taking, but he didn't say anything.

My parents gave me some money, and I spent some of my Macaw money on the supplies. I guess that made sense, because my parrot picture was the reason Mr. Collins asked me to join the art club in the first place.

Then when we were checking out, the man at the counter smiled and said, "I imagine you're going to be quite an artist someday." "No," I said, "I already am." I don't think that was a funny thing to say, do you, God? But the man and my dad both laughed. They weren't mean about it, but I don't like it when people laugh when I'm being serious.

Love,
Danny

WEEK 3

Monday

Dear God,

I just looked at my clock, and you are not going to believe this! It is 3:09 in the morning. I think that's a.m. I keep getting a.m. and p.m. mixed up. That's because it can be p.m. when it's still day outside and a.m. when it's dark.

I don't like being awake when everyone else is asleep. I don't like the way the house is quiet but not totally quiet—it makes all these funny creaking noises people don't notice in the daytime. I think the reason I woke up is that I'm so excited

57

about joining the after-school art club. Maybe I even dreamed about it.

Maybe I woke up because there is something lumpy under my pillow. It is a new canvas bag my dad gave me—as a surprise—to keep my art supplies in. I guess I should go back to sleep, or I will fall asleep in school tomorrow when I'm not supposed to.

I think it's good that you're always up, God. I would hate to be awake if you were asleep. But I know you never have to sleep. That seems so funny to me. It's hard to understand. But you don't mind that I don't understand, do you?

Good night, good morning.

Love,
Danny

Tuesday

Dear God,

This was a mixed-up day. Parts of it were really terrible, and parts of it were really good. The terrible part came after school when it was time for the after-school art club.

I had been nervous about it all day. I kept thinking, what if I get there and I have to go to the bathroom and I can't be excused? I checked my supply bag eighteen times to make sure I had everything. Finally Mrs. Whitney took it away from me for safekeeping, which is what she always says when she takes stuff away. I was worried that I wouldn't get it back, but I did, of course.

But the terrible part hadn't even started yet. I'm coming to that now.

When the bell rang, all the other kids

went one way down the hall to go out the door to go home. But I went the other way up the hall to go up the stairs to the upper-grade classrooms. I was halfway up the stairs, when I suddenly remembered that I didn't know where Mr. Collins's classroom was. So I walked slowly up and down the upstairs hall, trying to figure out which room it was.

The older kids were all rushing out of school, and I thought some of them looked at me funny, like they were thinking, "Who let that little kid up here?" I felt my face get all hot and my throat get all tight and sore.

By this time the halls were mostly empty, and I peeked in a room where the door was open, but there was just a small group of teachers talking. One of them looked up and asked if she could help me, but I just

60

shook my head because I was afraid my voice would get squeaky if I tried to talk. I thought to myself, it's getting late, and the club has probably started, and I can't walk in there after it has started. All the kids will turn around and stare at me. And what if Mr. Collins gets mad at me because I was late and says I can't join the club after all? But if I don't go, he'll think I'm not a nice kid, because he'll think I didn't want to join.

But sometimes the bad things I think are going to happen for sure don't happen after all. Because when I was walking up and down the hall, wondering what to do and praying inside my head for help, this older girl came up to me and said, "Excuse me, are you Danny?" I nodded. And she said, "Mr. Collins asked me to be on the lookout for you. He said he forgot to re-

mind you where the room was, and he felt terrible about that."

So it turned out OK, God. I felt like Diane (that's the girl who was on the lookout for me) was kind of a present from you. She said the club never started *right* after school, because Mr. Collins liked to wait for the noise to die down first.

They were just starting when Diane and I came in. Mr. Collins said, "Glad to have you!" He introduced me to the other kids, and they just said, "Hi," but they didn't look mean or anything. We got right to work, and I couldn't believe it when Mr. Collins said the hour was up and it was time to go home.

Before I left, I copied down the room number from the door because I didn't want to get lost and have Diane come looking for me again.

Isn't it funny, God? Going to art club was a new and scary thing to do. But now I've been there, and it will never be new and scary again. Are you proud of me, God? I think maybe you are.

Love,
Danny

Wednesday

Dear God,

When I got home from school today, my mom had some milk and brownies waiting for me. And she said she wanted to talk to me. Right then I should have known something was up.

She said my little triplet preschool girl cousins are coming to visit. For a *whole week!* My mother said my uncle is going to a sales conference in Hawaii, and he got a chance to take my aunt with him. My mother said my aunt needs a rest. Well, I can believe *that! I* need a rest with those three little kids running around.

"When are they coming?" I asked, thinking it would be sometime next month.

"On Saturday," said my mother.

Saturday! I told my mother she could at

least have given me more warning, but she said she didn't want me getting all worried and upset. And I said, "Who's upset? It's just doomsday, that's all. They'd just better not mess with my stuff." But all my mother said was that I should hide my stuff where they couldn't find it. What I want to know, God, is, why should they even be looking for my stuff in the first place?

That's the trouble with my cousins. They are everywhere. I don't mean that they're everywhere the way you are, God. I mean they keep popping up in all these dumb places. You know what they remind me of? Frogs. Miss Jenkins told us in Sunday school about the time the Egyptians wouldn't let your people go, so you sent frogs all over the place to make the Egyptians change their minds. When the Egyptians opened a cupboard, out jumped a frog. When they looked in a mixing bowl, there was a frog.

Suzy and Sally and Sammy are like little girl preschool triplet frogs. They crawl under the table to play house. And they like to scrunch down behind the couch. And one time I even found one in a closet when I opened the door. My mom thinks they are *so cute*. She never pays any attention to me when they're around. I'm just lucky I get any food.

And that's another problem with my cousins. Why do they want *me* to pay attention to them when they already get so much from my mother and father? But they always want me to play with them. It's very annoying, God.

My mother says my cousins think I'm special. I always thought I wanted to be special—like Curtis or something. But I think being special depends on who thinks you're special. Do you know what I mean? I would like to be special on a baseball team, but I don't want to be special playing house with three little kids.

I'm going to call Pug and tell him to come over when Suzy, Sally, and Sammy are here. He can bring his little sister Cindy. She is little, but she's still older than my cousins. And she can pretend she's their mother or something so Pug and I can go play.

I know this sounds like a crabby letter, but I feel *chrome yellow,* and I can't help it. I feel chrome yellow, because I hate that color. It's the color of school buses and

street signs and curbs. I don't have anything against those things, but I *hate*
chrome yellow, and this is a *chrome yellow
day.*

Love,
Danny

Thursday
Dear God,
This turned out to be *another* chrome
yellow day. That's because sometimes
when you tell people something, they don't
answer the way you want them to.

Mrs. Whitney has this thing she calls
sharing our experiences. It's really Show
and Tell. You get to talk into this microphone that really works and tell the class
your news. I was next in line, so I told
about Suzy, Sally, and Sammy. I explained
that their real names were Suzannah, Sa-

rah, and Samantha, and that they were my little preschool triplet girl cousins.

And the more I told about them, the more Mrs. Whitney just smiled and nodded. And when I couldn't think of anything else to say she said, "They sound just darling! Perhaps your mother could bring them by so we could meet them."

I think when you have awful news and no one thinks it's awful, that makes you feel even worse. Like, if you went up to the microphone and said, "I have to go to the hospital," or, "My dog died," Mrs. Whitney and everyone would say, "Oh, that's terrible news." But when you just say, "My cousins are coming for a visit for a whole week," everyone just says, "Oh, that's nice!" Well, it's *not nice*. It's *chrome yellow*.

It's bedtime now, and my father was just here to talk to me. It's the kind of talk

69

where mostly he has something to say, and I'd better listen if I know what's good for me. He told me he didn't like the way I was sulking at supper when he and my mother talked about my cousins coming. (I don't think I was sulking.) He said he knows it's not easy for me having three extra kids around, but he wanted me to promise that I would be nice.

I said I thought I should just promise to

try to be nice. But he said that wasn't good enough—he wanted me to promise to *be* nice. But I said all I could do was try, because what if Suzy, Sally, and Sammy did something really awful? I said I would try to be nice, but I couldn't guarantee anything because they were like little frogs all over the place and they'd better stay out of my stuff.

My father just looked at me like he didn't understand a word I was saying, and he just sat there rubbing his forehead. Finally he said, "All I want, is that you'll be nice to those three little girls." And I said, "I can *try* to be nice, but—" So my father said, "Oh, please. Not again." Then he said it was OK if I just promised to try to be nice as long as I tried my *level-headed best*.

So I said OK. I'm tired of thinking about my cousins, God. Sometimes when I talk

71

about something too much or think about it too much I get the same kind of feeling I get when I chew a piece of gum too long. It gets boring.

Love,
Danny

Friday
Dear God,
   You'll never guess who stopped by the after-school art club! Well, I guess you already know. I keep forgetting that about you. Anyway, *I* was surprised to see Pastor Bennett there. It turns out he is a friend of Mr. Collins, and he came by to bring back a book he borrowed. It's funny. I don't think of grown-ups having friends the way kids have friends, but Pastor Bennett and Mr. Collins are friends. I wonder if Pug and I will be like that someday? Mr. Col-

lins goes to a different church. I didn't know Pastor Bennett knew anyone who doesn't go to Apple Street Church, but I guess he does.

Pastor Bennett stopped by my desk and asked how I was getting along with Huey, Duey, and Luey. He meant my cousins, of course, and I thought that was pretty funny. I guess Mary Jo must have told him my cousins were coming. Pastor Bennett sometimes says Mary Jo is triplets. But she's not, of course. He just means she has enough energy and stuff for three kids.

I told him Suzy, Sally, and Sammy were coming tomorrow—doomsday. Pastor Bennett said you want us to be kind—even to people who drive us crazy—and that you help us do it, because it's so hard. He sounded serious, so I just said OK, I'd try to be kind. And he winked at me and left.

73

I think the other kids were surprised that Mr. Collins and I could be friends with the same person.

> Love,
> Danny

Saturday
Dear God,
Well, my cousins came today—right on time, wouldn't you know it. My uncle and aunt dropped them off on their way to the airport. My aunt kept looking like she was going to cry. I don't know why she looked like that if she was going on vacation. The kids had this big grown-up suitcase with their stuff in it. But each of them had a little toy suitcase, too. And there they stood in the hall with their little suitcases, and I thought my mother was going to die over how cute they looked.

74

My mother didn't want them to start crying about their parents leaving, so she took them into the kitchen for cookies and milk. And she told me to take the suitcases upstairs to their room. See what I mean, God? It's the start of my not getting any attention around here. That's how it goes. They go off to get food, and the slave carries the bags upstairs. I suppose I should go down to the kitchen to see if there are any crumbs left for me.

Love,
Danny

WEEK 4

Sunday

Dear God,

Today was Sunday, and if you think the ladies at church make a fuss over Mary Jo, you should have seen them with Suzy, Sally, and Sammy! They kept saying to me, "You must be so happy to have your cousins around—especially when you don't have any brothers or sisters." But just because people think *they* would like to have my cousins around doesn't mean *I* want to have them around, too. Sometimes I think I would like to have a brother. But three little preschool triplet girls? For-get it.

Pastor Bennett asked me how the kids were behaving, and I said they were OK and that they hadn't done anything awful so far—they were just being pretty quiet. I have to go. My mother just called me for lunch.

Love,
Danny

LATER

Forget what I said before about my cousins being OK and kind of quiet. Ha! I'm up in my room again, because my father sent me here to cool off. He says I *overreacted,* whatever that means, but I don't think I did. Here is what happened, God.

Dinner was OK, except my mother and father spent the whole time cutting up meat for the triplets and telling them to drink their milk.

78

After dinner I went into the living room to read my book. And my cousins were scrunched down behind the couch, only I didn't know that. Then they jumped out and yelled, "Boo!" and started giggling and giggling. The worst part of it was my mother and father started laughing, too. They said I looked like I was going to jump out of my skin. And I said I wasn't scared, just annoyed. But I couldn't get anyone to believe me. And that really made me mad.

So my father sent me to my room to cool down, and that's where I am now. I don't know if I am cooled down yet or not, because I didn't think I should have to cool down in the first place.

Love,
Danny

Monday

Dear God,

Well this is another day, and I'm back in my room to cool off again. And I'm too mad to write anything.

LATER

I'm not too mad to write anything now, but I'm still mad.

Those dumb triplets snuck into my room when I was at school and started playing with my toys. And the worst thing—they got into my paints and crayons and made a mess and broke two of my crayons and wore down the points on a lot of them. When I got home and found them, I screamed at them, but they just looked at me. My mother heard me, and she came running. And I showed her what happened.

80

Then my mother told the triplets they weren't supposed to go in my room and play with my stuff. She said it very nicely, but they started crying because they thought they were getting yelled at by their aunt, which is worse than getting yelled at by your mother—because mothers are supposed to yell, but aunts are supposed to be nice all the time.

But I wouldn't exactly call it yelling when my mother said, "Now, girls . . ." So I started yelling again myself, and my mother told me to stay in my room and cool off. This is getting to be an unpleasant habit, if you ask me. I mean, *I* didn't do anything wrong—*they* did. *They're* the ones who got into *my* stuff. And my mother just picks them up and tells them not to cry anymore—just because they say they want their mother. Honestly.

Just thinking about all of it made me too mad to write anything again.

Love anyway, I guess,
Danny

Tuesday
Dear God,

Well, *this* has been the most exciting day I can remember. Kids always say they wish exciting things would happen all the time, but when you have an exciting day, I'm not sure you want another one right away.

It all started when I came home from school and my mother said she had to run to the bank before it closed. She didn't want to load us all up in the car, so she told me to watch the girls and she would be right back. So there I was with Suzy, Sally, and Sammy, and, of course, they wanted me to play with them. I tried to call Pug to tell him to come over with Cindy, but all I got was a busy signal because his older sisters talk on the phone all the time. So it was just me and the triplets. And I figured I would show them how to draw, since they wrecked my crayons anyway. I made them sit in a row on the couch, and I told them I would be right back.

Well, this is the dumb part, God. I went upstairs to get the stuff, and then I saw this picture I was working on. I thought I would just fill it in a little more, and I guess I didn't keep track of the time. But then all of a sudden I remembered my cousins, so I grabbed the crayons and paper and ran downstairs because I was supposed to be watching them.

But when I got there, they were gone. I thought they were hiding to jump out at me again. And the funny thing is, when you think someone's going to do that, it makes you more nervous than if you don't know it's coming.

The first place I looked, of course, was behind the couch, but they weren't there. Then I looked under the table. Then I looked in all the closets.

By this time I was getting mad, but I was scared, too. I wasn't scared of them jumping out anymore. I was scared I wouldn't be able to find them before my mother got home. She might think I threw them out the window or something, and then I would get it.

I was beginning to think my mother should be home by now. And then the phone rang, and it was my mother. She said she had a little accident with the car—the kind they call a fender bender.

84

She said it wasn't serious, but she wouldn't be able to get home right away, and she wanted to know how I was doing with the triplets.

And this is another dumb part, God. I said they were fine, because I didn't know they *weren't* fine. I was sure I could find them before my mother got back, and now I had extra time because of the car accident. So I didn't tell her what happened, and I should have.

She said to keep a close eye on the kids, and I said I would. That wasn't exactly a lie, because I was going to keep a close eye on them—as soon as I *found* them.

When I hung up, I saw that the door was partway open, and I suddenly knew that the triplets were outside someplace. I didn't know how I was going to find them, and I was afraid they would get lost or run over by a car or something. And I prayed to you to help me. If you want to know the truth, I was kind of hoping you would send angels so they could fly around and see where my cousins were. But I didn't see any angels come, and I was really scared. I kept thinking of little places where my cousins could scrunch up, and I looked in those places first.

Then I heard a funny noise—like a bird crying, if they can do that. Then it said, "Help!" and "Danny!" And I knew it was my cousins, and I was never so glad to hear anything in my life. I said, "Where are you?" And they said, "Here!" which didn't help at all, but they were too little to know any better.

Finally I found them.

There's this little space between the toolshed and the garage, and they had

crawled in there and got stuck. And I think *I* do dumb things! I was so glad to see them, but I spoke to them like a grown-up, because that's what I was compared to them. I said, "You come out of there this instant!" But they started to cry, because they couldn't get out.

So I reached in and tried to pull them out. I got Suzy and Sally, but I couldn't reach Sammy. And I was too not-thin to go in after her. They just got more scared and started to cry louder—even the two who weren't stuck.

I kept wondering if some angels would show up, but all I saw was Curtis, riding down the alley on his bike.

I've always been a little shy around Curtis, if you want to know the truth, but this was an emergency. I called to him to help me, and he came right over. I explained what happened. I thought Curtis would know right away what to do, but the funniest thing was, he didn't. We both tried to get Sammy out, but we couldn't.

Then this idea got into my head. Maybe an angel dropped it in when I didn't see. And I said, "The fire department!" Curtis looked at me like I was crazy and said, "What fire? There's no fire." And I said, no, that one time when Mary Jo got stuck in the basement stairs, Mrs. Bennett had to call the fire department to get her out.

I was going to go call them, but the triplets started yelling at me not to leave. So Curtis said he would go. I told him not to go all the way to his house—just to use the phone in my house. I told him the number was by the phone, and Curtis went to call them. I told the triplets that if they would stop crying I would take them to the pet store to see a parrot.

And then I got another helper, because Julie came by with Oreo. She said she was taking Oreo for a walk, but she carried him the whole time. Julie said all Sammy had to do was walk backwards or turn around, which made sense, but Sammy was too scared to do it. But at least Julie got Suzy and Sally out of the way, because she let them play with Oreo.

Then Curtis came back, and pretty soon the fire department got there. They asked who called them and said it was good thinking. Curtis said he called, but that it was my idea, and the fireman looked at me and said, "Good thinking, son." He asked where my mother was, and I had forgotten all about her. But that was the very minute she drove up.

I guess you know that I had a lot of explaining to do. I never thought a person could be the hero and the villain all at the same time, but that's what I felt like. I think my mother was mixed up, too. She was mad at me for not watching the triplets and for not telling her everything when she called, but she was proud of me for hunting for them and for calling the fire department.

So the way it worked out, I didn't get a

reward, but I didn't get punished, either. Sometimes I guess that's good enough. Curtis and Julie are always the ones in charge, but I was the one who solved a big problem today.

Love,
Danny

Wednesday
Dear God,

Pug acted kind of funny today. I told him about the triplets and the fire department and everything, but he was mad that Curtis got to call the fire department instead of him. Then when I went to art club, Pug said it wasn't fair, that I'm special and I got to do everything. That's funny, because I don't feel special most of the time, and I never think I get to do anything.

But I guess I *do* get to do stuff. Because

92

in art club, Mr. Collins said that he was going to paint a mural on the basement walls of his church, and that any of us who wanted to could help. He said he was going to draw the outline and we could help him fill it in. I think I would like to do that.

Love,
Danny

Thursday
Dear God,

My cousins are so funny. All they can talk about was that I said I would take them to the pet shop to see the parrot. Kids! Honestly! You can't say anything around them, because they'll remember it.

My mother called and found out the pet store was open late tonight, so she said she would take us. The kids didn't know what a parrot was, so I showed them my painting. The girls wanted Julie to come with us, because they liked the way Julie let them play with Oreo. So I called Julie and she said it would be good for her to come, because she wanted to get a new toy for Oreo. If you ask me, that is one spoiled kitten.

So we went to the pet store. My cousins looked at the Macaw, but can you believe this? They were more interested in Julie and in the kittens than they were in me or the Macaw. Honestly! Who can ever figure out little kids?

So I got to talk to the store manager alone for a little while. He remembered me, which was nice. I hope he didn't remember how dumb I was. There was a sign on the Macaw's cage that said *SOLD*. The manager said the people were coming to pick him up tomorrow. That gave me a

94

funny feeling, God. I mean, I was glad the bird was going to have a home, but while he still lived at the pet store, I could sort of pretend he was mine in a way. Now he'll belong to someone else. I hope Pug's still not mad. He'll understand about the Macaw being sold, if he's not mad.

Love,
Danny

Friday
Dear God,

Today at recess I went over to play with Pug. I was afraid that he might still be mad about not being the one to call the fire department, but he seemed OK. And I was right—he did understand about the Macaw. I sometimes worry about what would happen if I didn't have Pug for a friend, but I don't think we'd stop being friends just because we get mad sometimes.

When I got home from art club, Pug and his little sister, Cindy, came over to my house. Cindy was supposed to play with the triplets while Pug and I went out collecting stuff. The triplets liked Cindy, but they still wanted Pug and me to play with them, and so did Cindy. So we all ended up playing together, and it was OK, I guess.

Pug and I started telling the kids about the times we were little like them. Pug told about the time he climbed way up to the medicine cabinet and ate some stuff just because he was curious, and he had to be rushed to the hospital and almost gave his mother heart failure. He told the kids, never, ever to do that.

I told about the time I got this paint set, and I decided I would invent a new color that no one had ever seen before. It would be the best color ever, because it would be a combination of all the other colors. But all I got was yucky brown. You know what, God? It's like I told the kids, things don't always turn out the way you think they're going to. Life is full of surprises, I told them.

Love,
Danny

Saturday
Dear God,

Today is Saturday, so of course I didn't have art club, but Mr. Collins said we could come to his church and help him paint the mural if we wanted to. My mother drove me over in the morning. It felt funny to go in a different church where the stairway and the bathrooms and the nursery and the kitchen were all in different

97

places. I could hear sounds coming from the basement, so I went down and some people were already there.

The mural was in the downstairs hallway. It was a picture of creation with all the plants and animals. Mr. Collins said he was glad I was here, because I could paint in the parrot.

Mr. Collins had drawn the outlines already, so all we had to do was fill in with paint. It was something like a giant coloring book, and it was a lot of fun. There were kids from the art club and people from Mr. Collins's church.

Some people from the church came in to make sloppy joes for lunch. So we had sloppy joes and potato chips and Coke and carrot sticks and chocolate cake. I was afraid I wouldn't have anyone to sit with, but I sat between Mr. Collins and Diane

98

from the art club, and the people from the church were really friendly.

Later I asked Mr. Collins if I could see the upstairs in his church, and he said OK. So we went up to look at it. It was bigger and fancier than our church. I thought about Mr. Collins and his friends being there on Sunday morning when I'm at my church. And then I thought about churches all over our town and the people who go to them. And then I thought about churches all over the country and all over the world. It gave me a funny kind of shivery feeling to think of all of us in church because of you, God. It wasn't a bad funny feeling. It was a good kind.

Something else happened today. My aunt and uncle came to get my cousins to take them home. It's funny. I forgot my aunt and uncle would be coming back. I guess I started thinking my cousins would be here forever.

My cousins were glad to see their mom and dad, but they were so busy playing, they didn't want to leave. I guess they thought they would be at my house forever, too. My aunt and uncle brought presents, which is a nice thing to do when people go away, I think. They brought me a Hawaiian shirt with Macaws all over it! I guess my mother must have told them I wanted a Macaw. Anyway, I will wear my shirt at home, but I don't think I'll wear it to school.

Then we all went out for pizza before my cousins left. We had a lot of fun. We had to get a big table in the restaurant. My mom and dad and I usually only need a small table. But it can be fun sometimes to have so many people you need a big table.

So anyway, God, this is later, and my cousins are gone now. And I don't feel like doing anything.

Love,
Danny

Sunday
Dear God,

Today at church all the ladies came up to me and said they bet I really missed my little cousins. I don't know if I do or not. All I know is, the house seems really quiet. Remember how I never used to think about that except when Pug says how quiet it is? Well, now I notice it without him telling me.

This afternoon I found this little tiny pink sock with lace around the cuff and a little blue and white and pink flower on it. Mom said she didn't know which one of the triplets it belongs to, but that she would put it in an envelope and mail it to my aunt. I still don't feel like doing anything.

Love,
Danny

Monday
Dear God,

Do you know what I noticed today? Sparrows aren't all one color of brown. The tops of their heads and their wings are darker brown than the rest of them, and sparrows have little flecks all over. Sparrows make me feel dumb for thinking brown is a yucky color. Sparrows are not as pretty as Macaws, but sparrows are pretty in their own way. I wouldn't want them not to be here. If all the sparrows turned into Macaws, that might be too much color. But you probably thought of that already, which is why you made the world the way you did. I think you did a good job.

This evening I went back to Mr. Collins's church to work on the mural some more. I told him what I figured out about sparrows, and he smiled like he thought I did some good thinking. Then I told him about my journal. I didn't tell him all the stuff I wrote in it, because that's private between you and me, God. But I told him that I wrote in it.

Then Mr. Collins told me that when he paints, he tries to please you with his art, and that's a kind of prayer. He said especially with the creation mural. It made him realize how wonderful you are to make the world, and thinking about you made him want to do his best work.

Near my parrot on the mural there are

104

some words, and I copied them to put in
my notebook, God. They say:

*Praise God from whom all blessings
flow.*
Praise him all creatures here below.
Praise him above ye heavenly host.
Praise Father, Son, and Holy Ghost.

Love,
Danny

If you enjoyed this book in The Kids from Apple Street Church series, you'll want to sneak a look at the diaries of all the kids in Miss Jenkins's Sunday school class.

1. Mary Jo Bennett
2. Danny Petrowski
3. Julie Chang*
4. Pug McConnell*
5. Becky Garcia*
6. Curtis Anderson*

*Available soon

You'll find these books at a Christian bookstore. Or write to Chariot Books, 850 N. Grove, Elgin, IL 60120.